Jack Ryder

I0547812

Tempted and Tamed

Corrupting the Choirboy 2

WARNING

This book contains sexually explicit scenes and adult language. It may be considered offensive to some readers. This book is for sale to adults ONLY.

Please store your files wisely where they cannot be accessed by underage readers.

* * * * * * * * * * * * * * * * * * *

WANT FREE COPIES OF MY BOOKS?
Just visit my blog and download free copies of my books:
jack-ryder.awesomeauthors.org/jack-ryder

About the Publisher

4Fun Publishing, a member of **BLVNP Incorporated**, 340 S. Lemon #6200, Walnut CA 91789, info@blvnp.com / legal@blvnp.com
NOTE: Due to the highly emotional reaction of some people to works of erotic fiction, any email sent to the above address that contains foul language or religious references is automatically deleted by our anti-spam software and will not be seen. All other communications are welcome.

DISCLAIMER

Please don't be stupid and kill yourself. This book is a work of FICTION. Do not try any new sexual practice that you find in this book. It is fiction and not to be confused with reality. Neither the author nor the publisher or its associates assume any responsibility for any loss, injury, death or legal consequences resulting from acting on the contents in this book. Every character in this book is over 18 years of age. The author's opinions are not to be construed as the opinions of the publisher. The material in this book is for entertainment purposes ONLY. Enjoy.

Corrupting The Choirboy 2

Tempted and Tamed

Erotic Seductions

By: Jack Ryder

© Jack Ryder 2015
ISBN: 978-1-68030-372-8

Chapter 1

Willow's mom was in the front pew when I stepped forward to sing the solo anthem hymn just before the sermon. She has been sitting there every Sunday since her divorce five months ago. It seems like her skirt and dresses have been getting noticeably shorter over the past several weeks.

Today, Gabi Pribino is wearing a very short grey sweater dress. Although it appears fairly acceptable when she's standing up, it tends to ride way up her thighs when she is seated. As the intro to the anthem is being played, I noticed that I can see the crotch of her white nylon panties. I feel a wiggle between my legs because they are transparent and I can clearly see her bare gash.

As I begin to sing the first verse of the song, I'm feeling very thankful that I wore a very tight jock strap today underneath my clothes. Last week, I got a full boner when she spread her legs to flash her crotch at me. Even with my tight jeans on underneath the choir robe, I was pretty sure that the folks in the front of the church might have noticed the bulge in my robe. Today, I was taking no chances.

I tried my best to not stare at her as I started the second verse. Gabi was smiling broadly as she very slowly spread her legs wider apart. I could very clearly see the pink folds of her pussy lips because her panties were now sopping wet. I felt my dick twitch as I motioned to the organist to stop after the refrain rather than go on to the third verse of the song.

As the congregation arose for the prayer before the sermon, I made my exit through the side door as always and practically ran to the changing room beneath the back of the church. I could feel the sloppy mess of precum in my jockstrap as I pulled my robe off over my head. I was just about to go into the restroom to relieve myself when I heard a chuckle behind me.

"I bet you go in there and jerk off…don't you?" The sound of Gabi's voice startled me. But the fact that it WAS Gabi's voice also sent a bolt of excitement through my rigid prick and I felt a small gush of warm fluid ooze into my pants.

"Oooh Geez," I gasped when I turned around to face her. Gabi was sitting on a wooden chair against the back wall. Her legs were spread apart and she no longer had her white panties on. "Do you like looking at my pussy, Jack?" she whispered. "Does it make you have naughty thoughts?" she purred. My dick was hard as rebar and throbbing painfully against my tight jockstrap.

"Yes…I mean…no…I don't have…nasty thoughts," I groaned. "So…You like looking at my nasty cunt but you don't wish you could shove your dick in it?" She goaded me with a wicked snarl. "Yes, I do," I blurted out as my face turned fire engine red. "I mean…Oh God…what do you want?" I moaned pitifully. Gabi was staring intently at the bulge in my jeans. "I want you to take it out and show it to me," she told me softly as she pulled her dress up to her waist to fully expose herself to me.

"But…what if someone comes and sees us?" I gasped timidly. I hated myself at that instant for staring at her dripping wet gash. And for the visions racing through my head of sucking on that pussy and then filling it with my rigidness. "We have half an hour until the service is over," she replied in a seductive tone as she dragged a finger all the way up her drenched slit. "Don't be a sissy," she goaded. "Let me see what a big boy you are."

"Oooooh Gaaaawwwwd," I groaned as I watched her bury two fingers into her pussy to the hilt. I was trembling as I unbuttoned my 501 jeans. My hands were visibly shaking as I hooked my thumbs in my jockstrap and yanked it down as well. *"I'm going to hell for this,"* flashed across my mind as I stood there in the basement of the church fully exposed to this gorgeous woman in the chair. My dick was bouncing against my belly with each pounding heartbeat.

"Look at you, Jack...You do like my nasty pussy," Gabi laughed in a nasty tone of voice. "Bring that over here and let me touch it," she purred. I was amazed that my feet started moving without any hesitation. I had to reach down and hold my jeans up as I made my way to where Gabi was seated. "That is sexy, baby," she whispered as she reached out to wrap her right hand around my dick. She had a curious little smirk on her face as she saw that her small hand barely made it all the way around my girth.

"Ooooooh...Fuuuucccck," I groaned as she slowly pumped her hand up and down my prick. "I bet you think about my pussy when you jerk off," she hissed her taunt. "Yes...I do," I mumbled hoarsely. "SAY IT THEN," she yelled. "I think about your pussy when I jerk off," I gasped without hesitation. "Good boy," Gabi chuckled. "And what do you want to do to my pussy?" she whispered.

"I...ugh...ugh...want...ugh," Gabi squeezed forcefully on my dick before I could finish. "SAY IT," she yelled.
"I want to eat your fucking pussy and fuck you till you can't walk," I screamed back. "Good boy," Gabi laughed wickedly. "Get on your knees and show me," she growled. "Maybe, if you please me, I'll let you relieve yourself," she added in a whisper. *I'm going to hell for this,"* my brain reminded me.

The strong muskiness of her sex burned in my nostrils and made me ravenous as I shoved my face between Gabi's legs and started sucking and slurping on her drenched sexhole. "Yes, baby...Eat me," she moaned as her head lay back against the wall. I reached up with my left hand and roughly squeezed on her right breast through the fabric of her sweater dress.

"Oh, Yesssss, Jack," Gabi moaned when I slipped two fingers into her gash. "Do that...Do thaaaaaat," she purred as I sucked on her clit while ramming my fingers in and out. I could feel her body writhing in her chair as her hands grabbed both my ears so she could grind her pussy against my face. "DON'T STOP, DON'T...YOU...OOOH GAWD...OOOOOOH GAAAAWWWWD!"

As Gabi jerked and convulsed in her chair, I drilled my fingers in and out of her savagely until her entire body finally went limp. I finally sat up on my knees and smiled at her. My face was dripping with her pussy juice. "Was that okay?" I goaded her as she sat there panting for air.

"You earned a second chance," Gabi growled hoarsely as she gazed down at me. "Now, stand up and show me what you do when you think about my nasty pussy." He voice once again had that commanding tone to it. "Better hurry," she laughed. "I want to see you jerk yourself off for me." She told me. "Just think about how nice this nasty cunt will feel wrapped around that big delicious dick," she added in a seductive tone.

My dick was saturated by all the precum that oozed out while I was eating her pussy. My hand easily slipped up and down the entire length of my prick as I started to beat off for her. The kinkiness of jerking off in the church basement while staring at Gabi's bare pussy was overwhelmingly arousing for me. It took less than two minutes for me to reach climax. "Oh Yes, Gabi...Gawd yes...Gawd yesssss," I screamed as I began to ejaculate. Three thick wads of semen sprayed out of my dick and landed on the floor near Gabi's feet.

Before Gabi left, she got my cell phone number from me and told me she would arrange a night that I could come over. "I'll tell Willow that you asked about her." Gabi smiled as she said it. "But you'll have to please me a lot more before I'll let you bang my daughter," she added with a devilish grin.

"Better pull your pants up," she laughed as she started up the stairs. "You wouldn't want anyone thinking that you were doing something nasty down here," she added. My eyes followed her swaying ass all the way up the stairs. I felt a shudder as I daydreamed about shoving my cock up her gorgeous ass.

"Was that Miss Pribino?" The sound of Pastor Jim's voice startled me as he came down the stairs. "Well,

Ugh...yes it was," I replied sheepishly. I was in my knees wiping the mess of cum off the floor. "She, ugh, needed to ask...for something," I tried to sound casual as I wadded up the messy paper towel and tossed it in the trash. "Better be careful with that one, Jack," Pastor Jim advised. "I don't like to repeat rumors, but even if a few of them are true...you best stay clear," he told me ominously.

***

Mom was in the kitchen cooking dinner when I heard the phone ring downstairs. I could vaguely hear her talking as I came down from my room but couldn't quite make out what she was saying. "Miss Pribino just called," Mom informed me as I entered the kitchen. "She says that you are going to be giving some sort of singing lessons at her house this evening." I froze in my steps. "She said what?' I asked curiously. "She said she's having some of the ladies over from church and that you are going to make them sing."

The way that Mom said it made it obvious that she has no clue how Gabi expects me to make them sing. I had to bite back a chuckle as I envisioned what Gabi might have in mind. "She told me not to expect you home tonight," she turned towards me as she said it. "You make sure you keep your hands off that Willow." Mom pointed her ladle at me. "I've heard that she's quite a slut."

Again I had to bite my lip. Mom had no clue that it is Gabi that has been exposing herself to me. She could never dream of the nastiness that happened in the basement of the church just a few hours ago.

"That won't be a problem, Mom," I chuckled. "Willow is away at college," I reminded her. It really flabbergasted me that Mom saw nothing strange about me spending the entire night with a very attractive older woman. But I certainly wasn't going to let on that there was anything to worry about.

Dad seemed a little more aware of the provocative situation. "You be sure to dress right when you go to bed," he advised me. "Don't you dare embarrass yourself by flirting with that woman," he snarled. "You behave like a respectable young man," he added with a stern look on his face. "I don't want to hear any bad reports from that nice young woman," he warned me. I had to bury my face in my pillow when I got to my room to muffle my hysterical laughter. Dad would shit if he had any clue what had happened in the church basement. Or any inkling of what was probably going to happen tonight.

Chapter 2

I felt a wonderful giddiness as I drove over to Gabi's house that evening. Although I really had no idea what she had planned for the evening, I was fairly certain that it would be nasty and sexual in nature. It was only an eight block distance from Dad's house to Gabi's. But it seemed like an eternity driving there.

I was greeted at the front door by Marissa James. She had been one of my Sunday school teachers way back when I was in elementary school. My mouth fell wide open as she stood there in the doorway. "The girls are waiting for us in the basement," she greeted me as I stood there staring at her.

At 43 years old, Marissa is a stunningly beautiful redhead with a voluptuous 38DD-30-36 hour glass shaped body. Her milky white skin looks smooth as cream and her soft auburn hair falls almost to her waist. Marissa is wearing a red transparent baby doll nightie with matching transparent red panties. My dick is swelling as I gaze up and down at her gorgeous naked body through the transparent fabric. "Let's not keep them waiting," Marissa chuckled merrily. Her words snapped me out of my trance and I stepped into the house.

"Ooooh, Gaaawwwd," I moaned softly as I followed Marissa to the stairs leading to the basement from the kitchen. The panties were a G-string type so I could clearly see her entire creamy white ass swaying back and forth in front of me. I was filled with an overwhelming desire to bend Marissa over and nibble on that delicious rear end.

"The guest of honor is here," Marissa announced as we came down the stairs. There were five more women waiting for me in the basement including Gabi. They were all women from my church. But I also recognized them from other activities. Carol Cummins had been my music teacher in Jr. High School. Barb foster was a Girl Scout mother who sold cookies in my neighborhood at the grocery store. Jill Adams was a little league mother whose son was on my baseball team. And Gail Goodwin is the present director of the church choir. She is the youngest woman in the house at 28 years old.

"Ooooh, Fuck Me," I groaned to myself as I glanced around the room at the women gathered there. They were all wearing identical baby doll nighties except in different colors. There were two long couch pit units in the basement. One on each side of the room which was about a thirty foot square room. In the center of the room there was a lone wooden chair that had a soft pad on the seat. I would be thankful for that with the events that were about to follow.

This will be your seat for tonight," Marissa informed me softly as she led me to the wooden chair. "But you must strip naked first," she added just as I was about to sit down. There were three women seated on each of the two couch pits. As I slowly began to remove my clothes, Marissa went over and joined Gabi and Gail on their couch. Gabi was already fondling Gail's breasts and kissing the side of her neck when Marissa joined them. She promptly pulled Gail's top down and began sucking on one of her exposed breasts.

I had very slowly pulled my tank top off and removed my shoes and socks. "Oooh, baby…look at that gorgeous ass," Carol gasped as I wiggled my jeans down. I did not wear any underwear that night at the request of Gabi. "Look at thaaaaaaat," Barb groaned as my dick sprang up and pulsated against my belly.

As if on cue, a huge strand of precum oozed out of my dick as I kicked my jeans off to the side. "I am so lucky," Jill gasped as her eyes followed the strand of cum till it landed on the floor between my feet.

After I sat down on the wooden chair, Gabi came over and told me to place my hands back behind the chair. As she handcuffed my hands together, she informed me that this would be about the women having pleasure. "You are just our toy for the evening," she whispered in my ear. "If you make us happy, I just might put in a good word to Willow," she reminded me. Jill was walking towards me with a huge grin as Gabi stepped away.

"We all drew straws for the exact order that we will have you," Jill told me as she stood over me with her legs straddling my knees. "I drew the lucky first straw," she added as she bent down just far enough to grasp ahold of my throbbing prick. "Where do you suppose I should put this, baby?" She had leaned forward to whisper it in my ear. She was rubbing her tits back and forth against my face as she said it.

"In your pussy," I answered very timidly. "SAY IT THEN," she yelled as she straightened up and let go of my dick. "Put it in your cunt...I want to fuck you," I shouted back. I heard chuckles and giggles from the women on the couch. SMACK...Ooowwwww," I groaned. I had not noticed the leather strap in her hand.

There was a searing pain in my left nipple that she had just slapped with the strap. But there was a huge gush of precum that oozed out of my dick at the same instant.

"Don't make me ask you something twice again," she growled. "Do you think I'm pretty, Jack?" she asked softly while she pulled the nightie off over her head. "I think you're sexy as hell," I answered her without hesitation. As I glanced around the room, I saw that four of the women were having sex with each other as they watched us and waited their turn to have me.

It took several moments for me to locate where Gabi had gone. She was over near the stairs. She had a very large professional looking video camera in her hand. She was recording everything that was happening in the room. "Oooh, God you're gorgeous," I gasped softly when I glanced back at Jill. She was now completely naked in front of me and standing directly over my pulsating rigidness.

"Did you play with yourself when you used to do sleepovers with Pete?" Jill whispered it as she reached down and guided my dick to her drenched slit. "Yessss, Mrs. Adams...yessss," I moaned as she slowly lowered herself till my dick was buried inside her sloppy wet cunt.

"Did you think about me when you were jerking off?" she moaned softly while grinding back and forth on my prick. "Oh, God yes! I did, I did," I groaned. "Did you want to make a mess in my pussy?" My entire body was trembling with arousal now. "Oooh, Fuck yes, Mrs. Adams. I want to fill you with my sperm," I moaned.

I could feel Jill's body jerking as she began to climax. I bent my head forward and sucked hard on her left nipple and nipped at it with my teeth. "I'm cumming. Baby...I'm cumming," Jill screamed while she pressed her tit harder into my mouth. Although I did not squirt inside of Jill, I was very pleased that she got off and I was happy that I would still be rigid for whoever would be next.

To my delight it was Gail that was next in line. When she got off the couch, she did not bother to pull her top back up. She came over and straddled my lap, yanked her G-string panties to the side and sat straight down on my slick wet cock. "Oooooh, Geezus that's good," Gail moaned once she was impaled on my dick.

"I bet you don't know that I never wear panties under my choir robe on Sundays," she whispered in my ear. "Sometimes, I'm completely naked underneath," she added as she began to bounce up and down on my rigid pole. "I bet you fantasize about fucking me," she whispered. "Oooooh, Gawd yes," I replied.

And that was the absolute truth. I have been fantasizing about banging her since she became the choir director two years ago. I had often thought that she was braless in her robe. I could often see her hard nipples poking against her robe. "I want to cum in you Mrs. Goodwin," I groaned. I felt her shudder as I said her name. "I've fantasized about this too," she moaned as she slammed down harder and harder.

I suddenly noticed that Gabi had moved closer with her video camera. She was recording a close up of Gail's pussy humping up and down on my dick. "Give it to me, Jack...Cum in my pussy, cum in me, baby,"

Gail moaned in a deep throaty voice. As her body began to vibrate into orgasm, my dick erupted and sprayed three ropes of semen deep into her womb.

There was a slurping sucking sort of sound as she lifted off of my dick. Gabi zoomed in to record the glob of semen that oozed out of Gail's gash. Then she moved closer to record the mess all over my dick. "I hope you're on the pill," Gabi laughed. "Maybe I want a baby," Gail teased her back as she glanced down at the river of semen oozing out of her. I felt an ooze of precum as I envisioned Gail's belly all swelled up with my baby inside.

Gabi then announced that we would be taking a twenty minute break so she could set up her massage table in the center of the room. As she unlocked the hand cuffs holding my arms behind the chair, she told me that she would leave me untethered on the massage table. "But you still must do as we say and you must not try to get off the table," she warned me. "Otherwise, we will tie your hands and feet to the table legs," she added.

Chapter 3

The women all crowded around me while we took our break. I was showered with hugs and kisses as we ate our snack of finger sandwiches and chips. Gail made it a point to tell me that I had the biggest cock she has ever had inside of her. She also told me secretly that I would be welcomed at her house anytime I may want to come over to play.

I could see Gabi gazing over at me with a sly grin as each of the women whispered little invitations in my ear. Jill invited me to take her to a drive-in movie. She told me she hasn't had sex in the back seat of a car since she was in high school. Carol told me that she'd love to take me shopping so we could sneak into a dressing room to have sex. Barb was the most brazen. She announced that she wanted to take me to the Adult Arcade and fuck me in the theater while all the men watch and jerk off.

"Looks like my friends are gunna be wanting more of you," Gabi teased me as she led me to the massage table in the middle of the basement. "Just don't forget who has the first claim," she added as she smacked my bare ass. "And don't forget the reward for making me happy," she whispered in my ear.

"Willow is such a young pretty little thing." I felt a shiver as Gabi sucked on my earlobe. "Just imagine how tight her pussy will feel around your big fat cock," she whispered very softly.

Once I was laying on the table face up, Carol and Marissa informed me that they were going to fuck me together. The massage table was adjusted down towards the floor till Carol could straddle my face standing up. It felt marvelous to have my dick swelling to erection in Marissa's mouth while Carol gently humped her pussy against my mouth.

It did not take very long for Marissa to have my dick hard as a brick. After she yanked off her G-string panties, she crawled up on the table and lowered herself onto my rigid prick till I was buried to the root.

"Ooooh, God that's good," she purred in a deep husky voice. It was electrifying to watch Marissa and Carol kissing and fondling each other as they tag teamed me. They were both grinding back and forth on me while moaning loudly.

Marissa was the first to climax. I could feel the pressure building up in my balls as she jerked and convulsed on top of me. Just as I was about to blow my load, Marissa lifted off my dick and scooted back towards my knees. "OH MY GAWD YES...FUUUUCCCCCK YES," I screamed as Carol bent forward and took my dick into her mouth. My cock ejaculated several huge wads of thick salty cream into Carol's greedy mouth. When she finally let go of my prick, Marissa leaned forward and kissed Carol very passionately. It took me a couple of moments to realize that they were swapping the load of cum back and forth between them. "Ooooh, gawd that's nasty," I moaned hoarsely.

***

While we were again resting, Gabi brought her cell phone over and handed it to me. "Willow is on the line," she told me as she slipped the phone into my hand. "I think I've convinced her to agree to a date," Gabi informed me. My hand was trembling as I took the phone. This is the girl I have pined over since elementary school. She is the sexiest girl I have ever seen. She has always had too many other boys on her arm to even approach her before this.

"Doesn't Jack have the sexiest ass you've ever seen?" My heart nearly leapt into my mouth as Jill said it. I was almost certain that Willow could probably hear the women in the background. "That fat cock filled my cunt better than any man I've ever fucked," Marissa answered her even louder. I had a sick feeling in my gut as I said hello. "This is, Jack," I announced sheepishly.

"Mamma says you were quite the life of her party tonight," Willow chuckled softly. "I can only guess what those horny old broads demanded of you," she added. "I hope it was fun for you too," she asked softly. "Yes…I had…a memorable night," I told her. After some small talk about how I have been lately and catching up with hobbies we both enjoy, Willow announced that she would agree to go to the drive in movie with me next Saturday night. She would be coming home from school for the 4th of July week.

"We'll see if we can make that memorable too," she told me before she hung up.

***

The other four women got dressed to go home while we were resting. Barb informed me that she and Gabi would be taking me on a road trip to complete the evening. When I asked for some clothes to wear, Barb just laughed and said I wouldn't need any. I was beginning to feel a knot in my stomach as I wondered where they would be taking me and the possibility of being seen naked. Most of me wanted to say no and call a halt to the sex game. But the possibility of being with Willow overrode my reasoning.

Although Gabi and Barb still had their baby doll nighties on when we walked out to Gabi's glossy black suburban SUV, I was completely naked. I practically ran to jump into the back seat even though it was past midnight. I could hear the girls chuckling as they climbed into the vehicle. "Poor baby's getting bashful on us," Barb teased me as she scooted into the back seat next to me.

"Nothing to worry about now," Gabi laughed. "No one will be able to see through my blacked out windows," she pointed out. Barb was already fondling my dick as Gabi pulled out of the drive way.

"You just sit back and enjoy the ride," Barb whispered as my dick swelled to erection in her hand.

"Ooooh, fuck me," I groaned when Barb leaned over and started sucking my cock right there in the back seat. I must admit that my dick got even harder as I watched cars whizzing past us on the highway.

Barb's tongue felt wonderful swirling around my dick. But she was obviously was just keeping me rigid.

Barb raised her head as we pulled off the highway and made our way down into the seedy part of downtown. "Don't worry, baby…you'll get some relief in just a few minutes," she told me as her hand continued to gently stroke my cock. Moments later, Gabi turned the suburban into an alleyway. It was the ally just behind the adult arcade.

As we drove down to the middle of the alley, I could see a couple of figures down towards the far end where the street light was not working. As the head lights illuminated them for a couple brief moments, I could see that there were two hookers squatted down giving blow jobs to a couple of men pressed back against the wall of the building.

"Okay baby, come to mamma," Barb purred as she laid back and yanked her transparent panties to the side. "Here? You want me to fuck you here?" I gasped softly. To add to my anxiety, Gabi was moving all of the windows down with the electric controls. "Yes baby, I want you to fuck me where I caught my ex-husband banging his hooker girlfriend." Barb pulled the front of her nightie down to expose her tits. My dick was so hard that I could not say no.

"Yesssss, baby…give it to me good," Barb moaned as I shoved my dick into her drenched hole till I was buried to the root. I saw the hookers stand up and wipe their mouths with the back of their hands. I saw the men pulling their pants back up as I hammered in and out of Barb's dripping gash.

Slap, slap, slap, slap…I'm sure the men could hear me pounding into Barb as they approached the SUV. When I glanced up front, I could see that Gabi had her panties yanked to the side and she was banging herself as she watched me fuck her best friend. "Need any help in there?" One of the men asked softly as they stood next to our open window.

Gabi leaned closer to the passenger side and chuckled. "No…we've got everything we need right here," she answered him. "We'd invite you to stay and watch but that would be pointless since you already relieved yourself," she added with a grin. I've gotta say that it thrilled me to have those two men standing there watching me fuck Barb.

I could feel the semen building up in my nutsack as the men leaned forward slightly to get a better view of Barb. "Give it to me baby, fill my cunt with your seed." Barb moaned it loud enough for the men to hear. "Ooooh, Fuck yes…Fuck yes," I groaned as my dick ejaculated three times while my legs vibrated uncontrollably.

"Yesssss, Baby…Yesssssss," Barb moaned as she got off too. Her eyes were glued to the two men staring in the window at her. My baby knows how to make his mamma happy," Barb told the men. "Oooooh, geezus," one of the men groaned. I could see Gabi jerking into her orgasm as the two men quickly walked away from the vehicle.

"One more stop, sweetie," Gabi announced as she pulled her panties back to cover her gash. It was at that moment that I noticed the video camera setting on the dash of the vehicle. The red light was still glowing red. Barb seemed thrilled with herself when she gazed down and saw the river of semen oozing out of her pussy. "Seems like baby boy enjoyed filling mamma with his seed," she taunted me. Barb bent over and kissed the head of my dick then climbed out of the back seat. "Barb will be driving us to our next location," Gabi told me softly as she joined me in the back seat.

It was a gated residence in the foothills that Barb drove us to. I was surprised that she knew the gate code to get us in the gate. "Willow told us the code," Gabi informed me while she slowly fondled my dick. "She comes to visit her Dad when she's home from school and he is often very late getting home," she added. Barb pulled the suburban in front of the two car garage so that the passenger side was facing the garage door.

"This is really gunna piss him off," Gabi laughed wickedly as Barb lowered the both windows on the passenger side of the vehicle. As I glanced up, I noticed a very large security camera attached at the top of the garage. From where it was located, it would easily record everything that happens inside of the SUV. "But....won't he see us?" I gasped as my dick became erect in Gabi's hand.

"You bet your ass he'll see it when he gets home tomorrow and checks his recording," Gabi laughed as she pulled down her nightie to expose her tits. "He'll see every minute of you fucking his ex-wife out in his driveway. "And he'll see me banging myself while I watch you do it," Barb added with a smirk. Gabi leaned forward as she tore her panties off and tossed them out onto the driveway. "Maybe, if you do a good job of it, Willow might let you bang her too," she whispered in my ear.

I pushed Gabi down onto her back and scooted up between her legs. "I'm gunna give you the best fuck of your life," I growled my reply as I rammed my dick into her to the hilt. "Oooh, God you're huge," Gabi bellowed as my fat dick stretched her pussy to the limit. I could feel her vaginal muscles quivering as I pulled out then rammed into her again.

"You like that big dick don't you," I taunted her loudly. "Yes...talk dirty...he'll hear that too," she whispered back. "SAY IT," I yelled. "YES...I LOVE YOUR BIG FAT DICK," Gabi yelled back. "Just think how good it will feel in your daughter's tight little cunt," I bellowed. I felt Gabi quiver when I said it.

"OH, NOT HER...PLEEEEEZE," Gabi moaned and began to thrash back and forth underneath of me. I reached down and pinned her head to the seat with both hands while she beat on my back with her fists. "Ooooh yes mamma, I'm gunna fill THAT tight little pussy with a gallon of my sperm," I yelled as I pounded down harder and harder. In the front seat, Barb was frantically banging herself as she listened to our lurid tale.

"TELL ME YOU WANT MY SEED," I yelled as I raised up with both arms to gaze down at Gabi. The expression of ecstasy on her face was amazing as she stared at me intensely. "GIVE IT TO ME...GIVE IT TO ME," she screamed her reply. "HERE IT IS," I hollered as I yanked out and crawled up her belly. "OPEN YOUR FUCKING MOUTH," I screamed just as the first ejaculation blasted out all over her tits. The second blast shot all over her chin and throat. Then, I leaned forward and the last squirt sprayed right into her mouth. "GOOD GIRL," I growled loudly.

I reached back behind me and shoved three fingers deep into Gabi's pussy. "Poor mamma needs some relief," I laughed wickedly. "Ooooh God, Ooooh God, Ooooh God....Barb was moaning in the front seat as she brought herself to climax. "Oh Yesssss...Do that....Do thaaaaaaaaat," Gabi shrieked as I drilled my fingers in and out of her gash.

I scooted back so I was sitting between Gabi's legs while I continued to savagely ram my three fingers in and out. One of my knuckles was crushing against her engorged clit as I reached forward to twist Gabi's right nipple with my free hand. "OH YES, JACK...GAAAWWWD THAT'S GOOD...GAWD THAT'S GOOD," she screamed as her body convulsed into climax.

Chapter 4

Gabi, Barb and I all slept together in Gabi's huge king sized bed that night. We didn't fool around anymore before we went to sleep since it was nearly 3am when we finally crawled into bed. But it felt incredibly wonderful to fall asleep between their two soft naked bodies. They took turns fucking me in the morning before breakfast. Gabi informed me that she would call later in the week to arrange another visit for me. "We can finalize your date with Willow," she added with a wink.

***

"You have some explaining to do, mister." Dad announced as he met me at the kitchen door when I got home at noon. I froze like a deer in the head lights and probably had the same expression on my face as well. "What?...I...What?" I stammered. "What exactly did you do last night?" Dad asked in a demanding sort of tone. "From what I've seen, it sure as hell wasn't singing," he added gruffly. My knees suddenly felt weak.

Before I could reply, Dad told me to follow him to the den. I could feel myself trembling as I followed behind him down the hallway. My mind was racing as I tried to decipher what he was talking about. Dad told me to close the door as he logged on to his computer. "Your mother would shit if she saw this," Dad muttered as he brought up a video screen for me to see.

The video feed was coming from one of the Cougar amateur video porn sites. I nearly jumped out of my skin when I recognized that the first five minute video was Jill bouncing up and down on me while I was handcuffed to the wooden chair. Although you could not see my face in the video, Dad had recognized the scar just under my right kneecap and the small birthmark on the inside of my left ankle.

After he showed all four of the five minutes videos filmed in that basement, he clicked on a second video link. There was a ten minute video of me fucking Barb in that alleyway behind the adult arcade.

That was followed by a fifteen video of me banging Gabi in front of her ex-husband's house. Although you could not see my face in those videos either, you could very clearly see the women's faces and most of their exposed bodies.

"Looks like you were pretty busy last night," Dad growled as he turned to face me. The room had been completely silent during the entire 45 minutes that he ran the videos. His sudden remark startled me out of my mesmerized shock. "I...don't know what to say, Dad," I gasped timidly. "I bet you don't," dad laughed as he sat back in his chair. "You fucked all six of those broads?" He asked in total amazement. "I...ugh...Yes," I confessed softly.

"Son...you are an adult now and have every right to do as you see fit," dad proclaimed in a stern tone. "But you really need to be careful about letting this shit get out onto the internet," he advised. Dad suddenly got a funny look on his face and stared intently into my eyes. "Give me that woman's phone number," he growled. "I want to have a word with her," he snarled.

There was a knot in my stomach as I wrote the number down on a note pad for him. "I really don't think she did anything wrong," I offered as I shoved the pad back to him. "She did give me the best night of my life," I added. "You are probably the only one on Earth that could have noticed my birthmark," I told him timidly. Dad then pointed out that there might be more footage where my face could be visible.

"You can go now," he dismissed me as he picked up the phone from his desk. My feet felt like lead as I left the den. I walked down the hall a few feet but returned to just next to the door once I heard Dad start talking. Although I missed the beginning of the conversation, I did hear him introducing himself to Gabi. "You remember me! The drab no-body who sat behind you in science class in high school?" After a slight silence he decided on a different tact. "Perhaps I should just say I am Jack's father," he growled.

There was another momentary silence and then he jumped in again. "That was absolutely irresponsible of you to expose my son to that sort of thing," he yelled suddenly. He was about to launch into a tirade as he often does once he gets on a roll. But he was cut short.

"What? Say that again?" he asked in a much softer tone of voice. "You....would do...that?" he whispered as if trying to believe what he was hearing. "Barb? The woman...from the alley way?" His voice had a quiver in it now. "Yes...that would be acceptable," he whispered. "I can be available then," he added. There was another pause and then Dad apologized for being so gruff. "Tell Barb I'll be delighted to see her...I'm sure we can work this all out."

I snuck into my room so dad wouldn't know that I was listening to his conversation with Gabi. I could hear him whistling in the shower as he got ready for his date with Barb. It sort of tickled me a bit to hear dad so happy. I noticed that his shower lasted much longer than usual. I also noticed that Dad had shaved and applied some of his favorite cologne. It was about a quarter till 1pm when I heard him leaving the driveway.

About ten minutes after dad left, I received a text message from Gabi. "Turn on your laptop at 1pm," it said. Then she gave me a private link to access. "You dad has a bigger surprise than he is expecting," she added at the end with a winking smiley face.

Mom was just getting home as I was about to make my way to my bedroom to log on to my laptop. I told mom that dad had gotten an unexpected business proposition. I made a mental note to inform him of the alibi so his story would be straight when he gets home. It was two minutes after 1pm when I joined the live link that Gabi had provided. "Holy shit," I whispered to myself when the live feed popped onto my screen.

Dad was sitting on the foot of the hotel bed in just his boxer shorts. The huge bulge of his erection was clearly visible tenting out his shorts. Barb was standing in front of him with her hands on her hips. She was wearing very tight black transparent yoga pants and a black chiffon blouse that was just tied closed with a loose knot underneath her breasts. I could clearly see dad's eyes bouncing up and down from her exposed tits to her pussy and back up.

"If you want the same pleasures that your son enjoyed with me, then you will have to do exactly what I tell you to do," she informed me with a growl. "Oh, God Yes...God Yes....anything," dad gasped his compliance. After Barb tied his hands and feet to the bedpost, she fastened a blindfold over his eyes. "This should make things more...fun," she laughed wickedly. "Is that okay with you?" she said it as she bent forward and took his dick into her mouth. "Oh, God Yes, God Yes," Dad moaned his reply.

Within a few minutes, Gabi had dad so aroused that his body was vibrating and his cock was pulsating against his belly as she stepped back from the bed. "I bet you'd like to feel some nice soft tits wrapped around this boner," she whispered. "Oh yes...Oh God yes," dad panted.

Just behind Gabi, I saw the bathroom door open slowly. "Oooh, Wow," I gasped softly as a young woman stepped into the room and quietly made her way to the foot of the bed. I did not recognize this woman with the platinum blonde hair that looked nearly pure white. I would guess that her perfect hour glass body is about a 34D-22-34. She is wearing only a white bikini bottom and nothing else as she bends forward to shove dad's cock between her perfectly round hooters. "Does that feel nice, baby?" She cooed in a soft husky voice. "Oh, God Yes...God Yes," dad moaned. He was so lost in his arousal that he could not notice that deep voice was not Barb's.

While the blonde woman began to slowly hump dad with her luscious tits, Barb quietly sat down in a stuffed chair next to the bed and began video recording the action with a camera she had sitting on the dresser. It was at that moment that I realized that the feed I was watching must be coming from a laptop on the opposite side of the room.

"I bet you want to shove this cock into my nasty little hole," the blonde purred. "Oh yes...oh please yes," dad moaned his reply. "Oooooh, Fuck Me!" I gasped when the woman dropped her bikini bottom to the floor. The blonde had a perfectly formed six inch dick that is fully erect and pulsating. "Oh gaaawwwd, look at that," I gasped.

As the blonde climbed onto the bed and straddled dad's dick, she reached back and pulled a small butt plug out of her rear-end. I could see a liquid glistening on the butt plug as she dropped it to the floor which means she has squirted some lube up inside her bum hole. "Oooooh God....that's incredible," dad moaned loudly as she slowly lowered herself onto his cock till it was buried in her ass.

The blonde was carefully holding her cock as she slowly rocked back and forth on dad's dick. I could tell by the way dad was moaning that her ass was milking his dick tightly as she humped him. She let go of her dick as she leaned forward. I could see it grinding against dad's belly as she rubbed her tits back and forth across his face.

"What's that...against my belly?" dad groaned throatily. "That's my nice hard dick," she told him softly. "Would you like to see it, baby?" She rubbed her tits back and forth against his face again. "Yes...oh yes," dad groaned hoarsely. The blonde reached forward and yanked the blindfold off and sat back up. "Oooh, look at thaaaaaat," dad gasped as he raised his head to get a good look at her pulsating prick.

"You like that...don't you?" the blonde taunted him as she began to stroke her cock while ramming her ass up and down on dad's dick. "Oh, Fuck that's hot," he moaned his reply. "If I untie your hands, would you jerk it off for me?" she offered quietly. "Oh, please yes...please yes," dad bellowed. I could see Barb smiling in the background as she continued to record every moment of the action.

"That's it baby…just like that," the blonde moaned as dad started gently stroking her cock. "Are you gunna fill my ass with your cream, baby?" she laughed as she quickened her pace. I could see that dad's body was quivering as she brought him closer and closer to climax. "Would you like to suck it, George?" she moaned. "Would you like to suck my dick?"

"OH FUCK…FUCK…OOOOOOH FUCK YES," dad screamed as he began to ejaculate. I could see the blonde rotating her hips as dad pumped his jism up her ass. "You gunna suck me dry, George?" she moaned as dad shot one last wad of cum up her butt. "OH YES, OH YES, OH YES," dad panted his answer. Without hesitation, the blonde scooted forward and placed the head of her dick into dad's mouth. "Oooh, Fuck me," I groaned as I watched the blonde hump her dick further and further into dad's hungry mouth.

I sat there in astonishment as I watched my dad greedily sucking the sexy blonde's dick. There were globs of thick white semen oozing out of her ass onto his chest as he gripped her ass cheeks to pull her further forward. "Joey has agreed to be your secret paly mate," Barb announced as she stood up and turned off her camera. "Your secret will always be safe with us…as long as our secret is safe with you," she added.

Barb was just leaving the motel room as Joey announced she was ready to cum. "Open your mouth and stick out your tongue," Joey moaned. "Don't swallow anything until I tell you." The first blast shot straight into his mouth. As she started to ejaculate for the second time, she laid the tip of her dick on his tongue and let the semen ooze out onto his tongue. "That's it baby, suck all my cream." She moaned as she shot off one last time.

"You like sucking cock, George…don't you?" she laughed wickedly as she sat back on his belly. "Now, show me all my messy cream," she taunted. Dad compliantly opened his mouth wide to show her the huge glob of sperm in his mouth. "Good boy," she laughed. "Now you can swallow it all," she told him.

Chapter 5

I waited until dad was in his car before I texted him to provide his alibi. "If you tell her Joey is a new business associate, that will help you with future...arrangements," I suggested coyly. In the back of my mind I could see the thick white jizz in his mouth and his sperm oozing out of Joey's ass. "Looks like you will be taking a lot more business trips," I goaded.

I met dad in the driveway when he got home. I reminded him to just act normal and carry on like any other day. I reminded him to not get too overly sweet with mom. "Women have a built in radar for that kind of shit," I told him. "Just be your normal self-absorbed self," I teased him. "Did you remember to clean out the garage?" He growled at me as we entered the house. "Yes, I cleaned up your mess," I goaded him with a smile.

I sort of cringed a bit when I saw dad feeling mom up in the kitchen while she was cooking dinner. But she seemed to enjoy the attention so I fought off the urge to crash into the kitchen and interrupt them.

I saw mom quiver as he mashed on one of her tits just as I backed out of the entryway. "Maybe tonight you'd like to get lucky?" she moaned softly with her head tilted back against his shoulder. While mom was cleaning up the dishes after dinner, I reminded dad that he should probably shower before bed. "It just won't be a good idea to go to bed with another woman's perfume on your body," I told him. "Or her semen all over your mouth and throat," I taunted.

It was just after 11pm when I received Gabi's text on my cell phone. I was pleased to get the distraction. I had been barraged with the deep guttural moans and the sound of squeaking bed springs for over a half an hour as my dad rutted into mom in the room down the hall. "You have a minute to talk?" Gabi asked. I didn't waste a moment. I pressed the ID photo of her cell number and then pressed call.

"Is talk all you wanted?" I asked playfully when she answered the call. The giggle that I heard from her end of the line told me she was pleased that I might offer more. "I contacted you to let you know that Willow is coming home early," Gabi informed me. "But I am available all night if you could find your way over here," she added. "I'll be over in ten minutes," I answered her.

Gabi met me at her front door nine minutes later. She was wearing a very short transparent red chiffon robe when she opened the door. Her naked body looked wonderful through the flimsy see through fabric. "I'm so happy we can have this time alone before Willow arrives," she greeted me as I stepped into the house. "After you've had her…you'll probably lose interest in me," she added softly. "Never in a million years," I whispered in her ear as I reached from behind to cup her breasts in both hands.

I was gently twisting on her nipples when she reached back to rub my dick through the fabric of my jeans. "I sure hope you feel that way after you bang my daughter," she moaned softly. I slipped one hand inside her robe to fondle her bare breast while I moved my other hand to rub her bare pussy. "I will always want this with you," I whispered. "No matter how many young girls want to fuck me." And that was the honest truth.

"Take me, Jack…fuck me right now," she moaned her reply. My hand was dripping wet when I pulled it away from her drenched slit. "You are my first lover," I told Gabi while I carried her to the couch. "You will always be the first no matter how many others I have," I pointed out. "You will always be the most special for me." I stepped back after laying her gently on the couch. "This will always be yours for the asking," I told her as I wiggled my jeans down exposing my rigid dick to her.

"Yessssss, that's it baby," I groaned as she leaned forward to suck my dick. Gluck, Gluck, Gluck, Gluck. As Gabi forced more and more of my fat dick into her throat, she gagged and a gush of saliva would ooze out and drool down onto her tits. It thrilled me to see the long gooey strands hanging from her chin down to her chest. "You will always be my nasty slut," I groaned as I gazed down at her messy chest.

After several minutes of this nasty deep throat blow job, Gabi's entire chest was coated with the gooey mess of saliva and precum smeared all over her tits. "I want you to fuck my tits," Gabi garbled as she lifted her face away from my throbbing prick. My dick was oozing a huge strand of precum and I stepped forward to shove my dick between her gorgeous jugs. "Yessss, fuck my titties," she moaned as I began to hump my dick between her tits with both hands pressing them together around my entire prick.

Squish, Squish, Squish, Squish…The sloppy sound of my dick humping her messy chest was exhilarating as I rammed my dick faster and faster into the deep furrow between her jugs. My legs were vibrating as I got closer and closer to climax. "Give it to me, Jack…Give it to me," Gabi moaned as she slid a hand up between my legs and pressed her middle finger into my rectum.

"OH, FUCK YES…OOOOOH FUUUUUCCCCCK YES," I screamed as my dick erupted the instant she shoved her finger up my ass. My dick spasmed four huge wads of thick juicy cream all over Gabi's throat and chest. My entire body vibrated as I watched the semen drool down her tits and then onto her belly. "You owe me a great blow job," Gabi chuckled as she gazed down to watch the mess running down her chest.

Gabi and I sat in her jacuzzi for nearly an hour after she tit fucked me on the couch. We kissed and fondled each other while we sat there and chatted. At eighteen years old, this is the most intimacy I have ever felt with anyone ever. "I love you, Gabi," I whispered in her ear as I groped her tits. "I will always love you," I added as I pulled her on top of my lap.

"Ooooh, Yes Jack," she moaned as I guided my dick into her sex hole. "You can love me all you want," she purred as she began to rock back and forth on my rigidness. I gently sucked on the side of her neck while she humped me. I tweaked her nipples and professed my love as I filled her vagina with my load of cum. "No matter what happens…you will always be my lover," I moaned softly.

While we were getting ready for bed, Gabi warned me that I should not confuse love with good sex. "We have an incredible sexual connection," she told me. "But love goes much deeper than that," she added.

I kissed her cheek gently as she rolled into bed next to me. "It's okay if you don't feel the same way," I whispered softly. "But I know what I feel in my heart," I added as I wrapped my arms around her and fondled her tits from behind.

"I didn't say I don't feel the same way," Gabi answered me as her hand came up to press my hand more firmly against her breast. "I'm just saying…it would be okay to love others too," she whispered. "I just want to be part of your life always," she added softly. I slipped my cock into her from behind and fucked her one more time before we went to sleep. "I want you in my life always too," I told her as we drifted off to sleep spooned together.

***

Gabi was on the phone as I quietly entered the kitchen in the morning. "You be nice to Jack," Gabi was saying just as I got to the entryway. "Even if you don't want to be with him, you be nice to him," she added sternly. "I will never forgive you if you hurt him," Gabi growled. I walked over to Gabi and held out my hand. "Let me talk to her," I told Gabi who was gazing up at me with a concerned expression on her face.

"Hello Willow, this is Jack," I announced. "Look…You don't have to bother seeing me at all if you don't want to," I informed her. "I know that I have never been your type of guy. I know that your mom probably put you up to all of this." It sounded like Willow was sniffling on the other end of the line. "I hereby let you off the hook, Willow," I announced. "I am very happy with the way things are without you having to compromise your own wishes." Before Willow could answer me, I handed the phone back to Gabi and left the kitchen.

***

I was just spreading some shampoo into my hair in the shower when I felt a cool breeze gust across my ass. "I think you misunderstood my conversation," Gabi announced softly as she closed the sliding door behind her. "You need to let Willow spend some time with you and let her tell you how she feels." Gabi was pressed against me from behind now. Her hands were roaming up and down my soapy slick body. "I think you may end up with two loves in your life," she whispered inches from my ear.

"Would you like that, baby?" she asked softly as her hand wrapped around my swelling prick. "Oooh, Fuck Yes," I groaned as she began to jerk me off from behind. I had to lean forward for a moment to rinse the soap out of my hair. Gabi took the opportunity to bend down and lick all the way up the crack of my ass. "Ooooh, Fuck," I groaned as my body quivered.

"I told Willow I would have you pick her up at the airport," Gabi mumbled between my ass cheeks while she continued to stroke my dick. "Is that okay with you?" As I was about to answer, Gabi burrowed her tongue deep into my ass. "Oooooh, Fuck Yes," I groaned. My legs vibrated so uncontrollably that I had to place my hands on the shower wall to keep from falling down. This caused me to bend over even further.

"My baby likes his ass reamed…doesn't he?" Gabi giggled. With her tongue out of me now, Gabi slowly slid her middle finger as far into my rectum as she could reach. "Oh fuck yes…fuck yes," I moaned as she wiggled her finger inside my ass. With her free hand jerking me off frantically now, I could feel the load of cum building up in my balls.

"You are gunna work all of this out with my little girl…aren't you?" Gabi growled. My balls were swelling with a massive load as Gabi leaned forward and shoved her tongue up my ass. "OH MY GOD

YES...YES, YESSSSSSS," I screamed as my cock began to ejaculate. Gabi continued to jerk me and wiggle her tongue inside my ass till I was completely spent.

I felt so light headed that I slowly crouched down till I was sitting in the tub with the warm shower water spraying down on me. "That wasn't fair," I moaned hoarsely. "Maybe not," Gabi laughed. "But it was divine...wasn't it?" she taunted. I nodded my head up and down as I glanced up at her. "Damn you're gorgeous," I groaned as I gazed at her wet naked body.

Even though I was too spent to become rigid again, I was filled with lust for this beautiful older woman who has become my willing lover. I crawled forward and lifted my face between her legs. "Oh baby...you don't have to...ooooh God yes." I could feel Gabi's body pressing back against the shower wall as I twisted my tongue as far into her pussy as I could force it.

"So good...s-o-o-o-o-o g-o-o-o-o-o-o-d," Gabi moaned as her hands came down to hold my head tightly against her gash. The sensation of the warm shower water raining down on me from behind felt very sensuous somehow. The water that was running down onto my face from Gabi's belly made it feel like she was wetting herself all over me. My dick quickly swelled back to full erection and I stood up.

"Oooh, Fuck Yes," Gabi moaned as I stepped forward and pressed my dick into her drenched slit. Bam, Bam, Bam, Bam...Gabi's ass slammed against the shower wall as I pounded into her savagely. I sucked on her tits while she wrapped her legs around my waist. Bam, Bam, Bam, Bam...I had aroused Gabi so much with my pussy eating that she reached climax very quickly. As her orgasm made her body spasm over and over, her clenching pussy muscles squeezed the semen out of my dick like she was yanking on a cow udder. "Now I can make up with Willow," I panted.

Chapter 6

I didn't recognize Willow at first as she made her way down the passenger ramp into the terminal. The last time I had seen her was at our graduation dance several months ago. Her long formal gown had been stunning and her long honey blonde hair had been professionally styled into many flowing ringlets that framed her angelic face and cascaded down her back almost to her waist.

There was a young slender woman walking down the ramp that I kept trying to see around as she approached. With the huge round sunglasses covering a large portion of her face, it was impossible to recognize that it was Willow approaching me. I remember thinking that I wished the hooker would get out of my way as I tried to see around her.

The slender woman was wearing a pair of extremely short white leather hot pants with a tiny white bikini top that you could clearly see through the black transparent half blouse that was tied loosely under her small perky breasts. The four inch cork heel sandals made her legs look sleek and muscular and made look like she as almost six foot tall. Her long blonde hair was in a single long ponytail that swished back and forth as she walked.

"Looking for something in particular?" Willow's voice startled me as I craned my neck to look around her. She had a wry grin on her face as my eyes darted back to look at her. "Damn! I thought you…were someone else," I gasped. I was glad I was able to cut off the part about thinking she was some hooker on the prowl. "You look…wow," I added as she stepped forward to hug me.

I could see many men in the terminal staring at us as Willow's perky tits crushed against my chest. It was a long and lingering hug and I could almost swear that she pressed her groin against mine. "We better go get my luggage," Willow whispered in my ear as my dick began to swell. It felt like she rubbed her crotch against my manhood just before she stepped back.

"We have a lot to talk about when we get to the car." Willow told me as she took my hand and pulled me towards the baggage claim area. I saw her eyes glance down at the bulge in my jeans several times as we walked down the exit corridor. I also noticed that there were a lot of heads turning as we walked past groups of men standing around gawking at us.

We found Willow's two huge suitcases within moments of entering the baggage area. It was a matter of pride that I carried both of her unbelievably heavy bags to the car. I was happy that the exertion had made my boner go away. I was also happy that Gabi had insisted that I use her Suburban SUV to pick up Willow. The extra room in the back with the lifting tail gate made it more manageable when it was time to toss the luggage into the vehicle.

I was breathing pretty heavily as I slid into the passenger seat after holding the passenger door for Willow as she climbed in. I enjoyed the view of her perfect little round ass as she bent over to place her purse on the back seat. I was smiling as I reached over to close my door next to me. Although my dick was only at half mast, it was still swelling.

"Whatever gave you the idea I wasn't interested in you?" Willow growled as she grabbed my shirt collar and pulled me towards her. Before I could answer, her lips were crushed against mine and she was forcing her tongue into my mouth. Because she had pulled me over so forcefully, I was still off balance as she French kissed me and I had to reach forward to keep from falling over any further. I felt my dick twitch when I realized that my left hand was now grasping Willow's right breast.

"I see that at least part of me interests you," Willow chuckled playfully when she pulled back to see me staring at her tits. "Although, I'm sure they are not nearly as interesting as my mom's," she taunted as she pulled back away from me. "Oh Willow...they...you are so gorgeous," I moaned as I sat up and forced myself to gaze into her eyes. "I have always thought you are the sexiest girl I've ever met," I confided.

"So, why did you think I'm not interested in you?" Willow asked again as she leaned back against the passenger door to face me. It was a struggle to not glance down at her perky tits as I started to answer her. "Because you have always had those bulky football jocks all over you," I responded softly. "Because you always seemed to want all of that attention." I added.

I lost the battle and gazed at her tits for a moment. When I glanced back up, Willow was smiling broadly and I could see that her nipples were pressing tightly against her flimsy bikini top. "You should have been more assertive, Jack." I flinched slightly when her left hand came over to rest on my right thigh. "I always flirted with you when I got the chance," she whispered.

My dick was quickly becoming erect as her fingers rubbed little circles on my inner thigh. "Yes…And every time I flirted back…one of your jock boyfriends would beat me up and humiliate me in the locker room afterward." I growled my reply. I could feel my cheeks burning from the embarrassment of telling her that. "I finally just gave up since I had no clue if you would ever be interested," I confessed.

"Listen to me," Willow told me softly as she leaned forward to be closer. As she leaned down a bit, the loose knot of her blouse came apart and the blouse fell open allowing me to clearly see both of her cone shaped tits. The fabric of the bikini top was so thin that I could see both of her puffy pink nipples through the thin white fabric. "I have always admired you ever since elementary school," she whispered.

"I have always wanted your attention." As she said that, she moved her fingers closer to bulge in my jeans.

"You can have my undivided attention now," Willow whispered as she moved her hand up to rub on my twitching bulge. "I might not be as good in bed as my mother, but I can give you things that she could never give you." My body shuddered as she squeezed on the head of my dick and a pearl of precum drooled out into my shorts. "I want to give that to you, Jack. I want that more than you can imagine." I felt another drool of precum ooze into my shorts as she rubbed her thumb back and forth against the head of my prick.

"Ooooh Gaaawwwd, Willow," I groaned as I felt a third gush of precum and my entire body quivered. "If you keep that up...I'm gunna cum," I groaned. Willow smiled wickedly as she began to pull open the buttons of my 501 jeans. "Would you like that, Jack? Would you like me to make you spurt?" she asked softly. "Oooooh, God Yes," I moaned as she reached into my shorts to pull my dick out of my open pants.

The fact that there were people walking around just outside of our SUV had me vibrating with arousal as I reached forward to fondle Willow's perky cone shaped tits. "Gaaawwwd, I want to fuck you," I groaned as she continued to jerk me off. "Not now, lover...I want the first time to be special," she cooed. "Gawd, you've got beautiful tits," I gasped after pulling her bikini top down to expose them. "Maybe you'd like to shoot all over them?" she whispered while she leaned down so my dick was right between them.

Squish, Squish, Squish, Squish...My dick was so lathered with precum that it made squishy noises as Willow stroked her hand faster and faster. I reached down and cupped both her tits in my hands and mashed on them as she jerked me right between them. "HERE IT IS...OOOOOH GAAAWWWWD YES," I screamed as I began to squirt my semen all over her creamy white breasts. "Ooooh, Fuck yes, Fuck yes," I moaned as I squirted a second time and then a third.

"That should hold you over till we get everything sorted out," Willow giggled as she sat up. I watched in amazement as she removed her bikini top and used it as a rag to wipe the mess off her chest. "I told mom that I would wait till after we settle things before I let you have me," Willow informed me as she put her black transparent blouse back on and retied the knot. "I don't want to be just a revenge fuck," she added. "Like I said...I've wanted you since grade school."

My hands were trembling as I put the SUV into gear to start our drive home. "You really mean it?" I asked softly. "You have wanted me since elementary school?" You could hear the amazement in my voice. "I'm so stupid," I sighed. "I never thought that for an instant." Willow reached over and patted me gently on the knee. "That's okay...all boys are stupid like that," she giggled. "And all the boys you don't want...are certain that THEY are the one you really desire," she added with a chuckle.

It was quiet most of the way home after that. I was lost in the amazement that this sexy young girl has wanted me as long as I have desired her. I was incredulous as to how all of this finally came to light. How her mother has seduced me into a sexual relationship that I could never have dreamed possible. And how Gabi was been the driving force to bring Willow and I together even though it could possibly end the affair between us.

"I don't know if I could ever stop seeing your mom," I confessed softly as we were turning into the driveway. "I have wanted you just as long as you've wanted this. But what happen with your mom is very special to me," I told her honestly as I shut off the ignition. To my surprise, Willow leaned over and kissed me very tenderly on the cheek. "I'm glad we settled that," she whispered in my ear. "I'll tell mom we have sorted everything out." I felt a shiver in my spine as her soft plump lips gently kissed the side of my neck. "You can have us both," she added as she pulled away.

As soon as we were in the house, Willow pulled Gabi towards the kitchen and told me to get comfortable on the couch while they make plans for dinner. Over the next several moments I heard whispering in the kitchen. Then I heard a little shriek that sounded like a squeal of joy. That was followed by some giggling and then more whispering.

It was Willow that came out of the kitchen first. "Mom is arranging for you to spend the holiday with us," she informed me went she joined me on the couch. "It seems that your dad may have an interest in smoothing that out with your mother," Willow whispered in my ear as she kissed my neck. "Mom told him that it would be a good opportunity to take your mom on a long overdue vacation." I shivered as Willow sucked gently on my neck. "Mom reminded him that Joey would be happy to welcome him back when they return."

Willow had her hand in my pants and was jerking me gently when Gabi came out of the kitchen. "It's all settled," Gabi announced cheerfully. "I'm gunna go shower and get ready for dinner," she added. "I'll leave you two some privacy." Willow had my dick out and was sucking me off by the time Gabi reached the bathroom door. Even though she didn't look back, I'm sure she knew what Willow was doing. It made my dick even harder as I felt the load racing to gush into Willow's greedy mouth.

Epilogue

I spent the entire four day holiday with Willow and Gabi. Although I spent each of the nights in Willow's bed, I did find some free time in the afternoon each day to satisfy my cougar lover too. By the time I drove Willow back to the airport on Sunday evening, the three of us had made our plan for the future.

We agreed that when Willow was at home, I would spend the majority of my time with her. But when she was away at school, I would stay with Gabi and I would be free to play with her friends as well.

I moved in with Gabi the day after Willow went back to school. It would be nearly two months before she would return for the Labor Day holiday. Although mom was none too pleased with the idea of me living with an older single woman, Dad managed to mollify her a bit by telling mom that since I was engaged to Willow, that it made sense for me to solidify my new family ties.

Dad was more than happy to do everything he could to smooth away any obstacles. His weekly visits with Joey had absolutely changed his life. Even his relationship with my mother had become more intimate since he sincerely wanted to keep her happy and satisfied. He confided to me that discovering that he was bi-sexual was the most exhilarating thing that has ever happened for him. I pointed out that the fact that Joey is gorgeous didn't hurt either.

When Willow returned for the Labor Day break, she informed Gabi and me that she was carrying my baby. There were tears and giggles and we had celebration that lasted well into the early morning. We called my parents at noon and invited them to follow us to Las Vegas for a quick wedding. Mom was crushed that it would not be a big fancy wedding. Dad managed to convince her that it was more important for us to be happy. The fact that he told her they could have another mini vacation seemed to be very agreeable to her as well.

I had Gabi bent over the couch in the dressing room pounding into her from behind with her dress up around her waist when dad burst in to announce that it was time for the small chapel ceremony. "Better hurry. Your bride is waiting," Dad growled. "I'm…Oooooh…cumming," I grunted as I flooded Gabi with my hot sticky seed.

I noticed that dad's eyes kept glancing down at Gabi's legs while Willow and I said our vows. He would tell me later that he could see a trail of semen running down Gabi's left thigh the entire time we were in the chapel. He confessed that he took mom upstairs and fucked her senseless as soon as the ceremony was over. I just laughed and told him I did the same with Willow.

--- END ---

Here is a sample from another story you may enjoy:

It felt embarrassing somehow to still be forced to wear this stupid black and white choir robe. The pastor informed me that the women's committee had insisted I wear it even though I only got up to sing solo during the noon service. That sort of creeped me out that a bunch of old church ladies wanted me to look like some young altar boy to sing a couple of hymns solo.

Margaret was sitting in the front row as she has since her divorce six months ago. She has made it a point to sit as close to me as she can. She has told me that she likes a good view when I'm singing. At first, I thought that she was just flattering me. But as time progressed, she has added little flirtations every week. If I wasn't so much younger, I would swear that she has been hitting on me.

At thirty eight years old, Margaret is still a smokin' hot redhead. She sort of puts me in mind of that "Lady Heather" character in the CSI TV series. Today she is wearing a very tight navy blue skirt. Although it is not exactly a miniskirt, it fits her so tight that I can barely keep my eyes off her gloriously sexy round ass each time we have to stand up.

Although her white blouse is suitable for church wear, it fits so tight that I can easily see the outline of both her 34D breasts. I can almost make out the edges of her areolas. But every time she leans forward, her blazer falls open enough that I get a good gaze at her tits. I find it curious that she has unfastened a couple of more buttons at the top of her blouse just before I'm about to get up to sing.

Pastor Boer was just beginning his weekly church calendar announcements. (Yes...that is really his name. He pronounces it BARE, but you can guess what most of us call him). As he was making a lame joke out of the mistake on the schedule that had been printed as pot-lick rather than potluck, Margaret leaned over just far enough that I could see most of her golden brown jugs. She was not wearing a bra and I could see most of both breasts except for her nipples.

I could feel a wiggle between my legs as I glanced up to find that she could tell where I had been looking. She was smiling as she reached over and gently laid her hand on my thigh. "Your singing always inspires me so deeply," she whispered as her fingers slowly grazed up my inseam. "I enjoy the view as well," she giggled softly. My body vibrated as a finger brushed across my now fully erect prick. "Go...inspire me,"
She chuckled just as the pastor announced my name.

I was actually really glad that I had the stupid robe on as I walked to the front by the choir loft. The robe would at least conceal the boner throbbing in my pants. I sort of had to slouch forward a bit so the robe would hang forward enough to cover the bulge. "Stand tall, sweetie," Margaret giggled softly as I turned to face the congregation.

Once Larry the organist started playing the anthem I had chosen, my dick went soft as I concentrated on the music. I deftly reached forward and quietly shut off the microphone. With my deep and bellowing baritone voice, I would not need it. I was nearly through the first verse when I made the mistake of glancing over at Margaret. She had a huge goofy grin on her face and her legs were spread wide apart.

The pastor always sits in a folding chair behind the pedestal pulpit while I sing. This way he is not a distraction and it gives him time to go over his sermon notes. It also blocks his view of the congregation. I was the only one in the church that could see that she was not wearing panties. I was the only one that could see her bare bald pussy.

I was so distracted by the muff shot that Margaret was giving me, that I accidently skipped to the 3rd verse of the song completely leaving out the second verse and the refrain in between. My face was as red as a fire truck as I walked back to my seat with the entire congregation looking at me with curiosity. I was also sweating profusely even though it was fairly chilly in the church. "Were you thinking something naughty?" Margaret laughed softly as I sat down.

To purchase the book, look for **Corrupting The Choirboy**.

Also by this Author:

The Wife Swap

In Love with a Cougar

Stella for Christmas

The Long Ride Home

A Shot at Love

My Swedish Greta

The Second Honeymoon

Candy's Playmate

Sara's House of Hands

Loving My Sitter

His Wife and Her Husband

Bi-Curious Couple

Take Three, Mr. Writer

Hired For Their Pleasure

Blackmailed Nanny

The Daring Doppelgangers

Serving the Therapist

Corrupting the Choir Boy

The Cheating Game

From the Author

WANT FREE COPIES OF MY BOOKS?
Just visit my blog and download free copies of my books:
jack-ryder.awesomeauthors.org/jack-ryder

If you have any comments, suggestions, or would just like to get a little personal, please feel free to email me at:
jack_ryder@awesomeauthors.org

If you enjoyed any of my books then please share the love and click like on my books in Amazon.

If you write me a review and send me an email I will send you a free book, or many.
(Just know that these emails are filtered by my publisher.)

Good news is always welcome.

One Last Thing, For Kindle Readers...

When you turn the page, Kindle will give you the opportunity to rate this book and share your thoughts on Facebook and Twitter. If you enjoyed my writings, would you please take a few seconds to let your friends know about it? Because... when they enjoy they will be grateful to you and so will I.

Thank You!

Jack Ryder
jack_ryder@awesomeauthors.org

About the Author

Jack Ryder LOVES everything there is about sex!

When he is not involved with his "swinger" friends, enjoying a steamy threesome, or being part of a raunchy "gang bang", you can find him on first class planes, trains, and cruise ships. Traveling seems to be the BEST way to finding new and interesting sexmates for him. Sexmates. Plural. He lives with the saying "The More, The Merrier!"

He owns a successful business in New York. He writes as a hobby and also as sort of documentation of his mind-blowing sexcapades over the years. He is presently roaming around the streets of Manhattan but can be anywhere in the world too, since he travels often. So, beware! You just might be his next mate.

*"The most fun thing I enjoy when writing my stories is trying to figure out which is fantasy and which was memory. ENJOY! (Preferably with a friend. *wink*) " -Jack Ryder-*

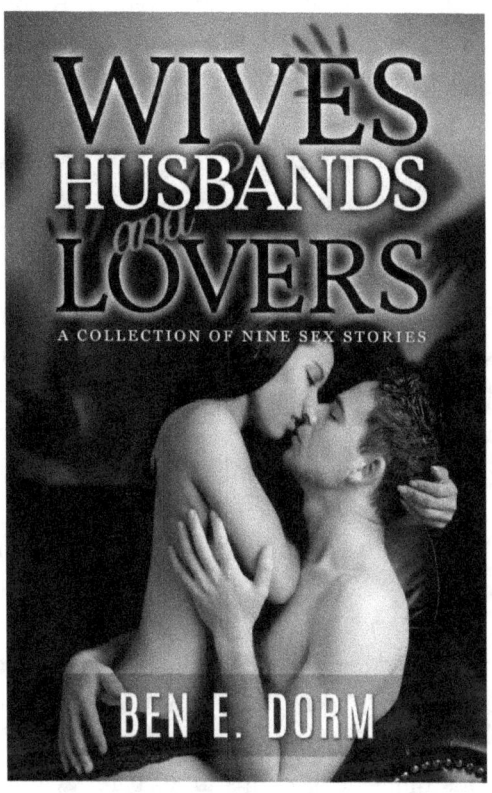

The audacity of the question caught Barbara by surprise. She blinks and gulps at her drink, then eventually splutters because she forgot it was wine in the glass. Swigging the stuff down like water was a mistake.

Struggling, Barbara stammers, "I... uh... I mean to say, Tuh-Tanya..." The heat rises in her face and she falls silent. Barbara doesn't have the words to respond. Her mouth hangs open while thoughts collide in a discordant jumble of conflicting impressions.

Everything is all furred up by the afternoon wine. *Dear God*, she thought, *it must be a bottle each by now!*

Barbara eyes, an offending article, a bottle of Sauvignon Blanc sat on the low table in front of her. Rather blurry, Barbara shifts on the very large, very comfortable three-seater sofa. She realizes that it's the third bottle, but it registers vaguely.

Slack-faced she lifts her face towards her host when Tanya cajoles her with, "Come on, Babs. Don't be shy. It's just a laugh."

Looking at the younger woman – who seems unaffected by so much drink – Barbara sees mischievous eyes twinkling in Tanya's elfin face. She takes in the detail of Tanya's platinum-blonde bobbed hair, dark roots visible in a central parting which, she believes, are the season's *de-rigueur*. She thinks dark roots are a particularly trampy look, but acknowledges Tanya carries it off well. In Barbara's estimation her host is a very pretty girl, but the understanding is slowly dawning and Barbara is coming to realize the innocence the young woman projects are rather misleading.

Barbara thinks the tramp style might be appropriate as she lowers her appraisal to Tanya's generous bosom beneath the tight, button-fronted blouse and smart, waist-length fawn jacket. A high-hemmed skirt rides up to Tanya's thighs, exposing a lot of bare, gym-toned and pleasantly tanned leg and Barbara is suddenly even more self-conscious when confronted with Tanya's physical appeal.

"Oh, Tanya, I don't know if that's entirely appropriate..." says Barbara, her tone stiff and pompous. She gulps more wine and wonders how the Liverpudlian girl can be so confident and self-assured, envy at Tanya's effervescence mixing in with what she perceives as her own repressed and strait-laced character.

Tanya's eyes roll as she says, "You won't shock me, Babs. I could tell you things I've done..." Then Tanya's glance flicks to Barbara's empty glass. "A top up?" she asks, reaching for the bottle.

"Oh, God, Tanya, I shouldn't. It's only three o'clock…"

But Barbara soon finds herself holding yet another brimming glass while Tanya grins at her.

"So, come on, Barbara," the blonde insists. "Tell me – what's the dirtiest thing you've ever done? Ever been to an orgy?"

Enough is enough, Barbara decides. "Of course not!" she gasps, bristling with indignation. "How absurd!"

Unfazed, Tanya laughs and continues with, "A threeway, then? Ever had two blokes at the same time?" Her expression turns vulpine, pale-blue eyes narrowing to match the sly grin Tanya fixes on Barbara. "A man and another woman?" Tanya adds, sipping wine, attention rapt and fixed on Barbara's face.

Barbara gasps again. "Tanya, please!" Her mouth opens and closes as she struggles with the disconcerting effects of afternoon drinking and the shocking interview. The wine combined with a totally unexpected line of questioning has her struggling for composure. This *isn't* what she's used to at all. "Why do you insist on embarrassing me?" she breathes.

Tanya laughs again before smiling at Barbara, her look contrite.

Holding up a conciliatory hand, Tanya says, "Okay, Babs, I'm sorry. I didn't mean any offense. I'm just a gobby cow. Always have been. I'm only teasin' ya."

It's the girl's accent, her blonde hair, the confidence and her youth that goads Barbara into revealing more than she knows is wise. Despite Tanya being at least fifteen years her junior, Barbara, at just over forty, feels so staid and unworldly – so bloody middle-class and *suburban*. She knows it's unwise but, fuddled with drink and confronted with

Tanya's supposed contrition, Barbara feels obliged to blurt her innermost and very intimate fantasies.

"Well," she says, voice low as she avoids Tanya's eyes, "if you must know…"

To purchase the book, look for <u>**Wives, Husbands and Lovers**</u>.

* * *

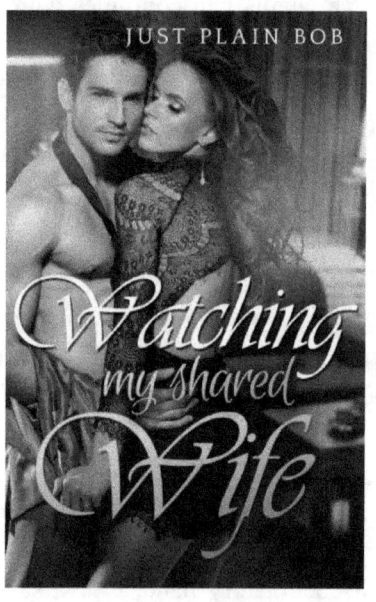

Wednesday morning at 8:13 is when my marriage ended. It turned out that we didn't need Glen to find out what Mandy was up to. Just the stuff that Hal planted in the house did the trick.

As soon as Mandy had left for work and I'd eaten breakfast I went to check the audio and video from Tuesday. The attic video showed Mandy downloading the receiver in what looked like a portable CD player. The camera in the living room captured Mandy coming into the room with a man I didn't recognize and they went over and sat on the couch. The man took Mandy in his arms and kissed her and then he asked her how much time he had. She told him that he needed to be gone by eleven and he said that he didn't think that would give him enough time. She giggled and said:

"You mean you still have something left after four hours in your hotel room?"

"I can never get enough of you and you know it."

"I just don't understand why you insist on making love to me here in my home and on my bed."

"Of course you do Mandy. You're mine and the best way to prove it is to have you here in your home, on your bed, your kitchen table, the washer and dryer, whatever."

"My husband just might have something to say about who I belong to."

"Fuck him! If he was strong enough to hold onto you I wouldn't be here."

"Would you like something to drink why I try and get you ready?"

"Scotch if you have it."

"Of course I have it sweetie. I knew you would be here so I made sure that I'd have your brand of scotch on hand."

"You knew I would be here?"

"Of course I did lover. I know what kind of man you are and I knew that sooner or later you would want me here. And don't give me any of that "I want you on your own bed" nonsense. You want me in my husband's house and on my husband's bed. You want to leave your smell in his house; take his wife in his own territory and don't you even try to deny it. Spread out and get comfy while I get you your scotch."

Mandy left the room and the man stood up, took off his trousers and briefs and then sat back down. He was stroking his cock when Mandy came back and handed him his drink. As he took a sip of his scotch Mandy went to her knees in front of him, leaned her head down and kissed the head of his cock. Then she licked the head and the shaft and took him in her mouth. She worked on him for several minutes and then he said:

"We need to take this to the bedroom baby."

"Your wish is my command lover."

Mandy got up and headed for the bedroom. By that time I had tears in my eyes. I loved that woman. Mandy had been my life from the day I first met her and I had spent the years following thinking that she felt the same about me. "Your wish is my command?" I was crushed. I forced myself to watch what took place in the bedroom. I was going to need some steel in my backbone for what was to come and the more I watched her betray me the harder that steel would become.

I watched as she lay back, smiled up at him and spread her legs wide. I listened as she moaned when he pushed his cock into her. I heard the cries and sounds that I thought I had been the only one to ever hear. I saw him finish, pull out and then move into a sixty-nine. I watched them lick and suck each other and then I watched him fuck Mandy a second time. I heard her tell him he had to leave.

"But why? He doesn't get off until eleven-thirty and he won't get home until after twelve. We have time."

"No we don't. I need to get these sheets off the bed and clean ones on and then I need to shower and douche before he gets home."

"Don't douche. I want to think of him feeling my cum on his dick."

"Oh sure, and what do I tell him when he asks why my pussy feels like a swamp? "Oh that? It's nothing. Just what my lover left in me." I don't think so."

"Just tell him that you are hot and wet because you got horny waiting for him to get home."

"You really want me to do that?"

"Absolutely!"

She was silent for a bit and then said, "Okay, but if it goes bad you may have to support me when he throws me out."

"You will do it?"

"Anything for you lover, you know that."

"If he catches on and splits you know my standing offer. I'll put you up in your own condo."

"That's sweet lover, but you do need to go, but be ready for my call if he doesn't like the feel of you."

I thought back to the previous night. Mandy met me when I came in the door. She was wearing a black lace nightgown, high heels and her make-up had been freshly done.

"I need you baby. I'm as horny as a goat and I need you. Come on baby, hurry to bed."

To purchase the book, look for <u>**Watching My Shared Wife**</u>.

* * *

Mary was fed up with being left behind each month while Riley went up to the cabin with his three friends, Mark, Robert, and John, to fish, drink and just have fun. She was only 23 and she wanted some fun, too. She resented being left behind to fend for herself in this way. She poured herself another drink, her third, and flopped down onto the sofa in frustration as she sipped her drink. *I'll show him*, she thought, sipping her drink, a plan coming into her head. Quickly gulping the rest of her drink down, Mary went to her room and quickly threw a change of clothes and some toiletries into a bag, grabbing her pocketbook and keys as she locked the door behind her and got into the car. If she drove steadily, she could be there in three hours and surprise them.

Mary had to stop a couple of times on the way as she felt herself getting tired, but she finally pulled up to the cabin around four in the morning. As she let herself in, she heard the sounds of snoring coming from different areas of the cabin. She was tired and felt a bit ragged from all she had drunk during the evening, so she quietly tiptoed to the bathroom to take a shower. The water felt so good after the long drive and she stood under it enjoying the sensation.

When she got out of the shower and dried herself, she appraised what she was seeing in the mirror. Her long red hair hung down to the middle of her back. She had that pale skin with light freckles that was common to redheads. Her breasts were very full with large pale nipples on the ends. Mary cupped them in her hands, gently squeezing them as her fingers automatically sought out and found her nipples, squeezing them and pinching them, pulling on them as they screwed themselves into large hard knots. Her hands trailed down her flat stomach to where a small thatch of bright red pubic hair used to grow above her pussy. She had no hair on her pussy, having had it removed by electrolysis so that it was as smooth as a baby's. At the top of her slit, her clit hood peeked through her pussy lips and her clit, fat as a pinkie finger, stuck out from beneath its hood. Her hand trailed down and her fingers trailed up through and between her pussy lips, feeling herself and the wetness that was starting. Her legs were long and straight, as were her feet and toes. Men had always found her beautiful and at the moment she quite agreed with them.

She was still squeezing her breasts with one hand, her other still between her legs when suddenly the door opened and Robert staggered in, completely naked, his cock dangling in front of him, bigger than anything Mary had ever imagined. As he shut the door, he blinked his eyes, trying to clear the fog of alcohol and sleep so he could make sense of what he was seeing.

"Mary?" he croaked, his voice still sounding a bit drunk.

"Hi, Robert," Mary said, frozen where she stood, her hands not moving.

"What're you doin' here?" he asked, slurring his words. "And how come you're naked?"

"Uh, I thought I'd drive up and surprise Riley and I just took a shower," she replied, letting her hands fall to her sides as she stared at his cock which was beginning to grow even larger...

To purchase the book, look for **Desired By The Boys**.

* * *

Thirteen years ago I joined a private dungeon group in Seattle, Washington and had attended several parties held there and had never met anyone like Mistress. It was a Friday night and the theme that night was take down play. I am not sure if you know what this type of play involves. In a nutshell, anything goes in this play. It is usually reserved for the most extreme playing or to teach someone a lesson that was not learned before.

I had a chance before to play with others as I come to the dungeon alone and the scenes always drew an audience. You see, I love pain...cannot get enough of it. It does not matter to me what is done as long as nothing is broken and I do not require a trip to the emergency room after playing. So the scenes I was involved with became quite messy with my blood from being whipped or having needles stuck into my most private spots and various other tortures I endured.

Tonight as before, I sought out the Events Director and told her I would like to play if someone was looking. I wandered about the room watching subs and slaves being put through their paces...hearing their screams...the sounds of whips and canes striking their flesh. I do not see many males here tonight and I like that as it meant I might have a better chance at the rough playing I needed.

My wandering brought me to the far corner of the dungeon where a very pretty woman about 33 was strapped face down upon a sawhorse type of apparatus with her wrists and ankles secured tightly along the legs of the horse. There were 2 men at each end of her, one ramming her ass and the other pumping her mouth with a steady rhythm going. There was a woman wearing a black leather corset and black garter with thigh high nylons standing next to them. This woman wore no panties and had a neatly shaved vagina that peeked out from under the garter affair she wore. As the men fucked the helpless woman on the horse, the other woman was whipping her hard across her back and shoulders. Her back was crisscrossed with dozens of stripes looking very red and some almost purple. Blood oozed from many of the whip marks.

I was so enthralled by this scene I was not aware the Event Director was calling my name. I kind of jumped a little when she touched me on my shoulder and I turned to see her standing there with another woman I had never seen before. She introduced her as Miss Sarah and left us alone. This woman was beautiful with long flowing dark brown hair and deep blue eyes. She had an ample bosom, tight waist, long, shapely legs. The most striking thing about her was the long elegant evening dress she was wearing. More suited to being at a fancy ball then a dungeon. Miss Sarah had been watching the scene I was and had a chance to watch my reactions also. As she stood beside me she asked my name and I replied, "Miss Sarah I am David". We talked for 20 minutes while watching the whipping continue and I was asked many questions about my likes and dislikes and what I hoped to find here tonight.

I told Miss Sarah what my limits were. While I did this I looked her in the eyes and I could almost see a fire glowing from inside her. I shrugged it off as my over active imagination playing tricks on me. Miss Sarah reached her hand out and stroked my broad chest and it was almost like being touched with an electric current. It took my breath away and I felt my knees quiver just a little. I had never felt this way from being touched before now.

Miss Sarah eyed me and watched my expressions as she asked if I really wanted to play with her tonight. I almost screamed out my answer but managed to hold back and told her, "Miss Sarah I would like to play with you."

She placed her hand in mine and walked away from this scene to the various restraint sections of the dungeon until we stopped at a huge wooden X shaped thing. The beams were 10 feet long and made of solid oak 8 inches square. Each beam had 12 eyehooks bolted into it and was impossible to pull loose from the wood. The top and bottoms of the beams were secured to the roof beams and wooden floor and would not tip over no matter how hard someone would struggle.

To purchase the book, look for **The Mistress And The Pet**.

* * *

MOLLY'S Daughter

LILITH JONES

After the lunch crowd had gone, Anne Bernard watched Mom from the window of the diner until she got to the house. Minutes later, Mom called that she was lying down.

Mom had handled the diner for years by herself. Anne hadn't appreciated how much work it was. Even when she had helped after school, she had bitched at how hard she worked instead of seeing the killing hours Mom had worked. And, then, she'd left Mom to handle it herself for three school years while she was in college. Mom had lied to her about the cancer when she was home for Christmas, though she could tell Mom wasn't feeling healthy.

Now, Mom still came in for lunch and dinner hours. It was Molly's Diner, and Molly still kept it up.

-=-

Greg Thibault shook the cell phone in his hand. He kept from throwing it across the mesa by telling himself that that would only make the situation worse. And a worse situation than the present would be unbearable. Every arrangement which had been "of course, Professor

Thibault," or "no problem, Greg," when he had been in Boulder was unraveling at the other end of an unreliable connection.

"Look," he said, "I'll call you back in an hour or two with better reception." He punched off. He didn't know whether the guy at the department had heard him, but they would know that he wasn't on the line.

The phone companies boasted that they covered 99% of the people living in the country. This mesa was in the 1%. To be fair to the phone companies, not that Greg felt like being fair to any phone companies right then, the Anasazi weren't actually *living* in the United States. The last of them had been dead five centuries now.

He gave elaborate instructions to his students, descended by the footpath, and headed out in his Jeep. He took a quarter hour to get to something paved. The Jeep was supposed to be an off-the-road vehicle. It's just that the mesa was further off the road than the Jeep had been designed for. He found that his AC was dead, but he would have to climb back up the mesa and down again to get the keys for another vehicle. He opened the windows and got hot, moving air.

He wondered vaguely just why he'd bothered with giving the directions. Being a programming executive described as "like herding cats." Supervising archeological graduate students was like that, but worse. Everybody knew how to do the job better than the instructor did.

The nearest cellphone tower was between the two small towns of Randolph and Copper City. Randolph, the closer one, was more than an hour away. Even so, he passed only three cars on his way. Archeology got done in dry, empty country. It wasn't that Minnesota hadn't had cultures living in the area for millennia; it was that most of their artifacts had rotted or sunk into the ground. When the Anasazi had tossed out a potsherd, it was still where they'd tossed it.

He pulled into the parking lot of a diner in Randolph and called again. His hassles had only begun, and he spent half an hour on the cell, mostly on hold. By then, sweat was running down his body and pooling in the seat of his pants.

Hot, still air was worse than hot, moving air. And the air down here was, if anything, hotter than the air on the mesa. He looked across at Molly's Diner. He had seen the air conditioner when he'd driven in. His glasses were too streaked with his sweat now, but he could hear it when he listened. He'd been an idiot. He would go in and ask to make the other calls from there.

He'd left before lunch. He hadn't missed much. Assigning cooking duties only to coeds would be arrant sexism. On the other hand, guys who were going to major in Anthro didn't take home-ec in high school. Most girls who were going to major in Anthro didn't take home-ec either. Or, if his present students had, they had forgotten everything they'd learned in that course.

The diner had an air conditioner. He could hear it. He'd eat and make the rest of his calls from there. He headed into the diner.

-=-

Anne didn't recognize the customer who came in. The non-local customers were truckers. How had an 18-wheeler got into the lot without her hearing it? The guy looked rugged, but not like a trucker, and she didn't know why for a minute. Then she did. He was tanned, deeply tanned, but the tone was even. Truckers had more tan on the left side.

She grabbed a menu, and the guy sat at the counter. She got behind the counter and handed him the menu. He took off his glasses and held the menu close.

"The home-made chile looks good," he said. "Might I have some of that?"

"Coffee?"

Greg shivered, and it wasn't the AC. That voice was the sexiest voice he'd ever heard. And she wasn't trying to be sexy. She had only asked if he wanted coffee.

"Please."

Anne poured him his coffee before getting the chile. Truckers, and many locals, were more interested in the coffee than in the food. She'd learned to brew good coffee. That meant pouring out a lot and alternating pots and scrubbing them often. A cup of coffee brought in more than making a pot cost, though, and truckers chose to stop based on the quality of the coffee.

Greg liked the coffee. The chile was the best-tasting food he'd had since he'd come to the mesa. Better than that, it tasted good. He got a napkin out of the dispenser and wiped off his glasses. The waitress was the sexiest woman he'd ever seen. And it was neither her attitude nor her clothes.

She was wearing a blouse that covered her to the elbows and an apron over that. He'd spent the last two weeks with girls wearing shorts and halters, and none of them had been so attractive. The waitress had long hair, but it was tied up in a bun with a pencil stuck in it.

She hadn't presented the bill, but he paid with a $20. She brought him back his change. She stayed within sight while he ate, and that was easy on the eyes.

"Look, ma'am," he said, "the air is out in my Jeep. I have some calls to make from this area. I've been working in a dead zone." He held up his cell. "Would you mind if I made them from that table back there?"

Anne said, "Go right ahead. Want more coffee?"

"Please." This guy had said please more often to her in the last ten minutes than some regular customers had in the last month. She couldn't figure him. He didn't have a local accent. Something in his speech reminded her of the professors at Tempe, though they hadn't been that polite. He looked like he sweated every day in the sun, and he sounded like he spent his life in a library.

He stood at the counter until she had refilled his cup. Then he carried it to a table by the door. By the air conditioner, too, she noticed.

He talked on his cell. He'd been right that he had *some* calls to make. After the second, he drained his cup and put it down. She carried the pot to his table to refill the cup.

"You didn't have to do that," he said. "I could have gone back for it."

"I wait tables."

"And cook?"

"And sweep the place out at night," she said. "This place barely supports Mom and me. It couldn't pay for a big staff." How barely it supported them, she wasn't going to tell a stranger, however nice he talked.

"Well, I don't know about the sweeping, but if you cooked that chile, you did a damned fine job."

"Why, thank you."

A trucker came in for coffee and pie just then, and she didn't pay attention to the guy until the trucker was served. The guy got loud on the phone towards the end, though, and she could hear that. Apparently, he could tell.

"A lady can overhear me, which puts a real crimp in my vocabulary. But you can take the next down handbasket." The person at the other end apparently said something. "No. Both of you are women, but only one is a lady."

After he closed the cell, he brought his cup to the counter for more coffee and ordered a hamburger. He waited there for the burger, paid, and waited for his change. The driver went out and the guy went back to his table. He made another call and argued some more.

Greg was perfectly well aware that yelling on the phone didn't make them hear you any better. Sometimes, though, he couldn't resist. Finally, he ended his last conversation with Boulder and closed the cell. He brought his cup and saucer back to the counter.

"What sorts of pie do you have?"

Anne said, "Peach, apple, and cherry. We don't cook the pies, though." She couldn't figure why she'd said the last. Just that the guy had said nice things about the chile.

"I'll risk some cherry, anyway. And more coffee." She got the coffee and the pie. He paid immediately, using some of the change she'd given him earlier. She suddenly wondered whether the $20 bill was all the money he'd brought with him.

Greg ate the pie slowly. He told himself that he wanted to stay because of the coolness. The waitress was great to look at, and great to listen to, though she hardly spoke to him. Still, she was a pretty girl in a town full of young men. She was certain to be taken. He could look, but not touch.

"You were right," he said, pushing an empty plate and an empty cup away. "The pie was not home cooked. Nothing wrong with it, though. This is a nice place, how long are you open?"

That, he thought, was real suave, Thibault, not! 'When do you get off?' Indeed. The question isn't when she gets off, but where you get off.

"We're open six to ten."

"Thanks." He put a couple of bills under the edge of his plate and walked towards the door. "Really, thanks for everything," he said before going out. It would be a long drive back, and into the setting sun, too.

Anne said, "You're welcome," in a voice which was probably too low for him to hear. Then she got his dishes, spoon, and fork into the soaking water. There wouldn't be many customers before supper. She might as well wash the dishes now, so she did.

She put the tip into the cash register. About half the truckers and a quarter of the locals tipped. Their tips seldom folded. Of course, the guy had eaten a lot, and he had asked about making calls from here. But people called on cells from the diner all the time. Two free refills weren't a lot, and he sure hadn't made her walk. She did hear his car leave, though she hadn't heard it arrive.

Well, she'd tell Karen about the mysterious stranger in September, and she would invent one of her marvelous stories to explain him. Then Anne stopped smiling. Would she go back to school in September? Would she ever see Karen again?

To purchase the book, look for **Molly's Daughter**.